For Mum & Dad

t

templar books

an imprint of Candlewick Press

First U.S. edition 2020

First published by Templar Books, an imprint of Bonnier Books U.K. 2019

Library of Congress Catalog Card Number pending

ISBN 978-1-5362-1016-3

20 21 22 23 24 25 TWP 10 9 8 7 6 5 4 3 2 1

Printed in Johor Bahru, Malaysia

This book was typeset in Amelia BT, Factura, and Futura Book BT.

The illustrations were created digitally.

TEMPLAR BOOKS

an imprint of

Candlewick Press

99 Dover Street

Somerville, Massachusetts 02144

www.candlewick.com

MOLLY'S MOON MISSION

DUNCAN BEEDIE

Molly the moth
lived in the back of a closet.
She loved her home and her family,
but she yearned for adventure.

"I want to be an astronaut and fly to the moon!" Molly declared.
"I'm not sure your tiny wings would make it there," said her mother.

We'll see about that, thought Molly.

So when she wasn't busy helping her mom look after her siblings . . .

she trained hard for her space mission.

At long last, she was ready!

5 . . . 4 . . . 3 . . . 2 . . . 1 . . .

BLAST OFF!

And to Molly's surprise,
a few seconds later . . .

"I made it to the moon!"
she cried.

"This isn't the moon," buzzed a huge fly. "This is a light bulb! The moon is much bigger and much farther away. Too far for a little mite like you."

We'll see about that, thought Molly, and she set off in search of a much bigger light.

"Oh, you poor little creature," said a large spider.
"This is a street lamp. The moon is much, much brighter
and much, much farther away.
Too far for a little thing like you, I'd wager!"

We'll see about that, thought Molly.
She flew on until she saw a light that was bigger and brighter
than anything she had seen before.

She followed the light around and around in circles.
The closer she got, the dizzier she became.

Eventually,
Molly was so dizzy
she fell to Earth with
a *plop!*

"I guess this isn't the moon either then," sputtered Molly.
"I'm afraid not," said a wise old crab as he fished her out of the tide pool.

"This is a lighthouse. The moon is much, much farther away."
"Too far away for a teeny moth like me, I suppose?" Molly asked sadly.

"I don't know about that," replied the crab. "I could count the number of fish
I've caught on one pincer, but it hasn't stopped me from trying night after night."

Encouraged by the crab's words, Molly patched up her helmet,
saluted, and launched herself upward once again . . .

toward the biggest, brightest, farthest light she could see.

After a long, giddy flight, Molly finally touched down.

"Surely this must be the moon!" she cried.

She wandered across the pale,
dusty landscape.

All of a sudden, home felt a very,
very long way away.

Just then, a giant shadow
loomed over her.

ONE SMALL
STEP FOR . . .
A MOTH?

"Hey, watch out!" shrieked Molly,
jumping out of the way in the nick of time.
"Sorry about that, kid!" said the astronaut.
"I didn't expect to find anyone else here on the moon!"

"You mean I actually made it to the moon?"
Molly asked. "I knew I could do it!"

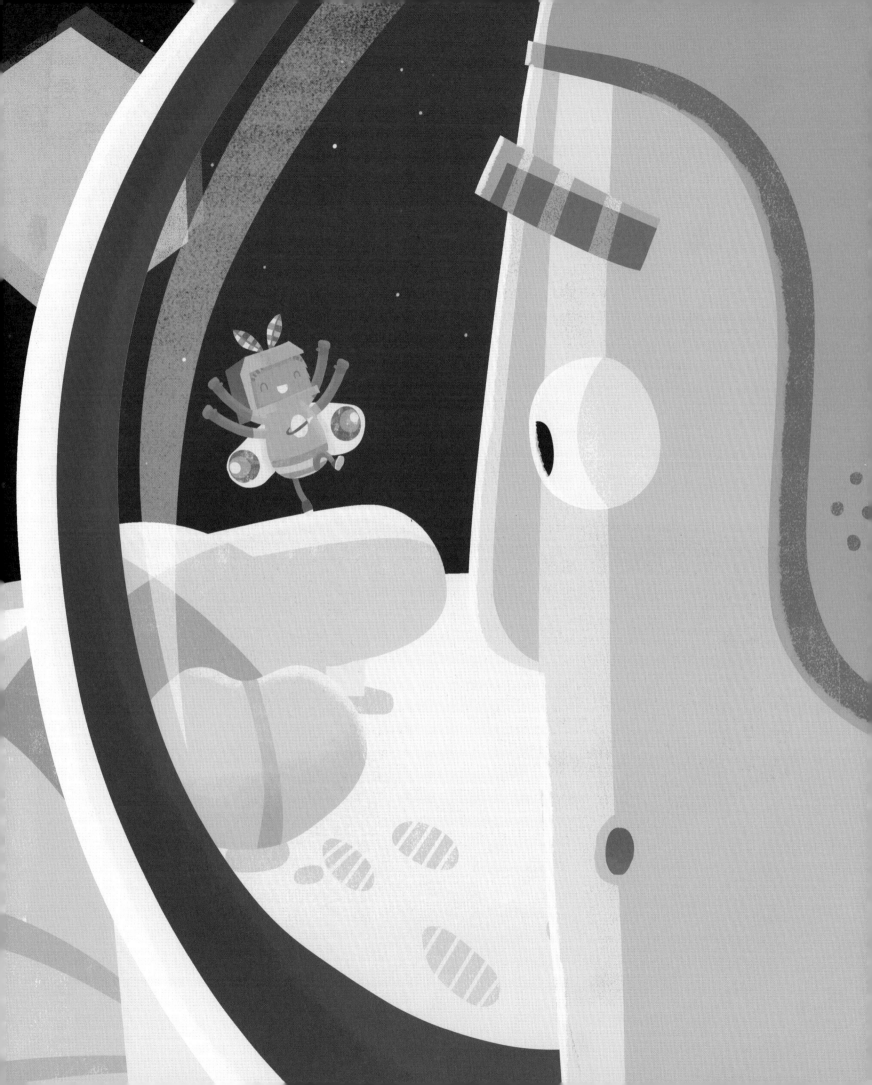

"That's a pretty giant leap for a little critter," said the other astronaut.
"I guess you'll be too tired to help us with our special mission then?"

"We'll see about that!" Molly said cheerfully.
So she helped the astronauts take photos of the moon's surface.

Then she helped them collect samples of rocks and moon dust.

And they even had time for some fun . . .

before planting a ceremonial flag.

"We'd better be heading back," said the astronauts
as they prepared the lunar module for liftoff.
Molly stared out into the vastness of space. It was so dark.
How would she ever navigate her way home?

"Cheer up! You're one of us now, kid!" the astronauts said,
and they gave Molly her very own lunar mission patch.
"Now, how about we give you a ride home?"

"Ooh, yes, please!" said Molly.

As the astronauts busied themselves in the module, Molly gazed out the window toward Earth.

Far away, the city lights twinkled.
But one of those lights was
bigger, brighter, and more inviting
than all the others.

And before she knew it,
Molly was safely back home.

"I've been to the moon!" Molly cried,
giving her mother a big hug.

"Well, I never!" her mom exclaimed proudly.
"My Molly, the only moth ever to fly to the moon!"

We'll see about that! thought Molly.

THE END

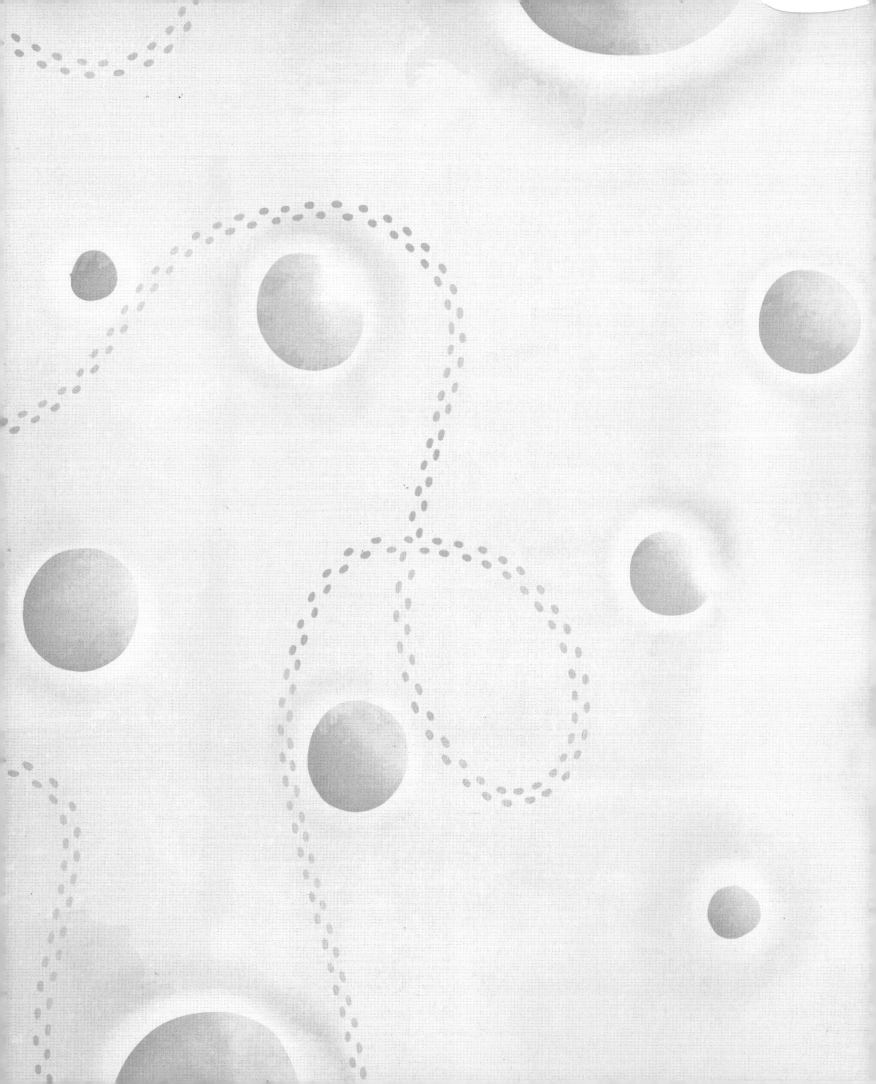